YOU ARE INVITED

Birthday Party

WHO: GRANDMA
WHEN: OCTOBER 24, 2016
WHERE: 257 CAPLAN AVE

About this Book

The illustrations for this book were done in pencil, crayon, watercolor ink, and Adobe Photoshop on 140 gsm Gold Sun woodfree. This book was edited by Bethany Strout and designed by David Caplan. The production was supervised by Erika Schwartz, and the production editor was Andy Ball. The text was set in Dantat and the display type was hand–lettered by the author.

For Kyle.
Be patient. We have
all the time in the world.

Bethany & David

The car trip to visit Grandma is always exciting!

But after the first hour,

it can feel like an eternity.

You might find yourself saying things like,

Are we there yet?

or,

This is taking forever.

Staring out your window at a thousand miles of road can get boring pretty quickly. Not even all the toys in the world can help.

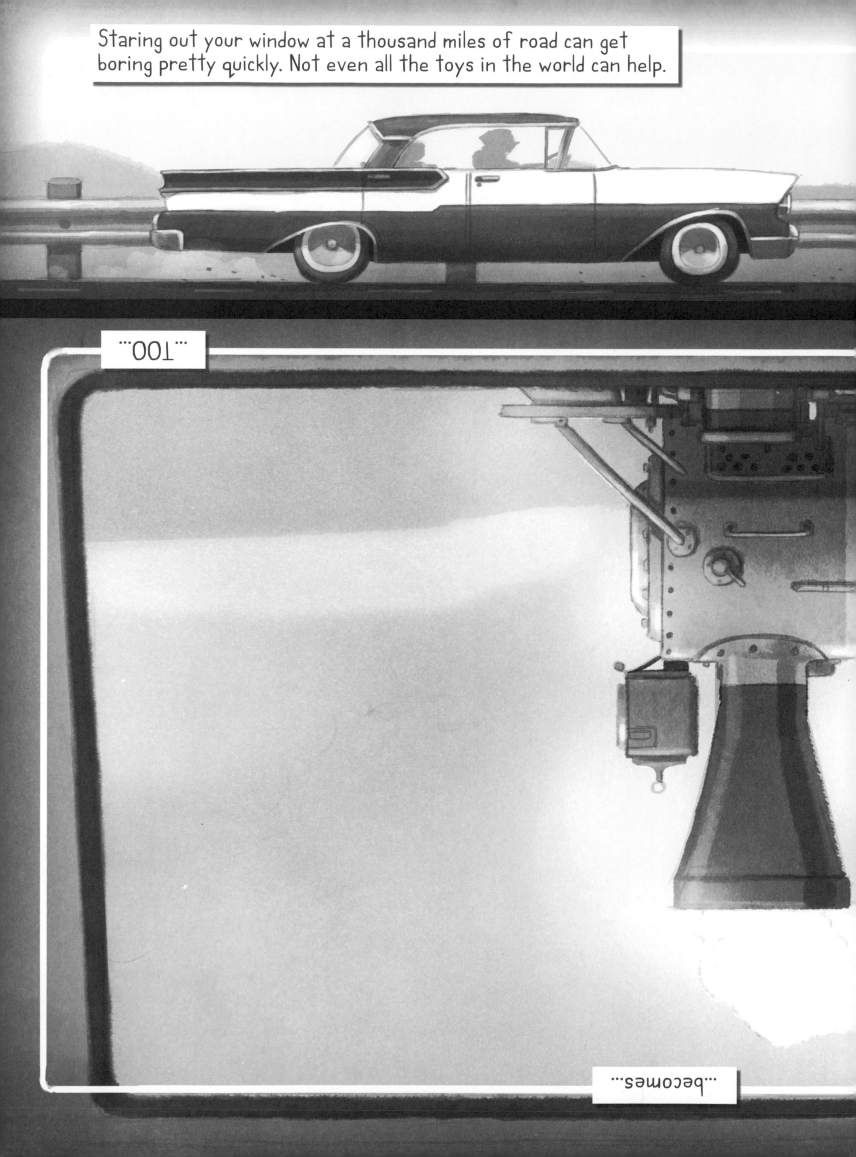

...TOO...

...becomes...

Minutes begin to feel like hours.

"This will just be a quick trip," your parents promised...
I have to go to the bathroom.
2BZK131

...but it feels like it's been a million years.

time fly by quickly.

So take a second to savor the moment you're in.

Maybe it will fly by too quickly.

257 Caplan Avenue?

That's Grandma's address.

The road is full of twists and turns...

And you...   ...never...   ...know...

...where...   ...life...   ...may...

...take...   ...you.

So sit back and enjoy the ride.

But remember, there's no greater gift than the present.

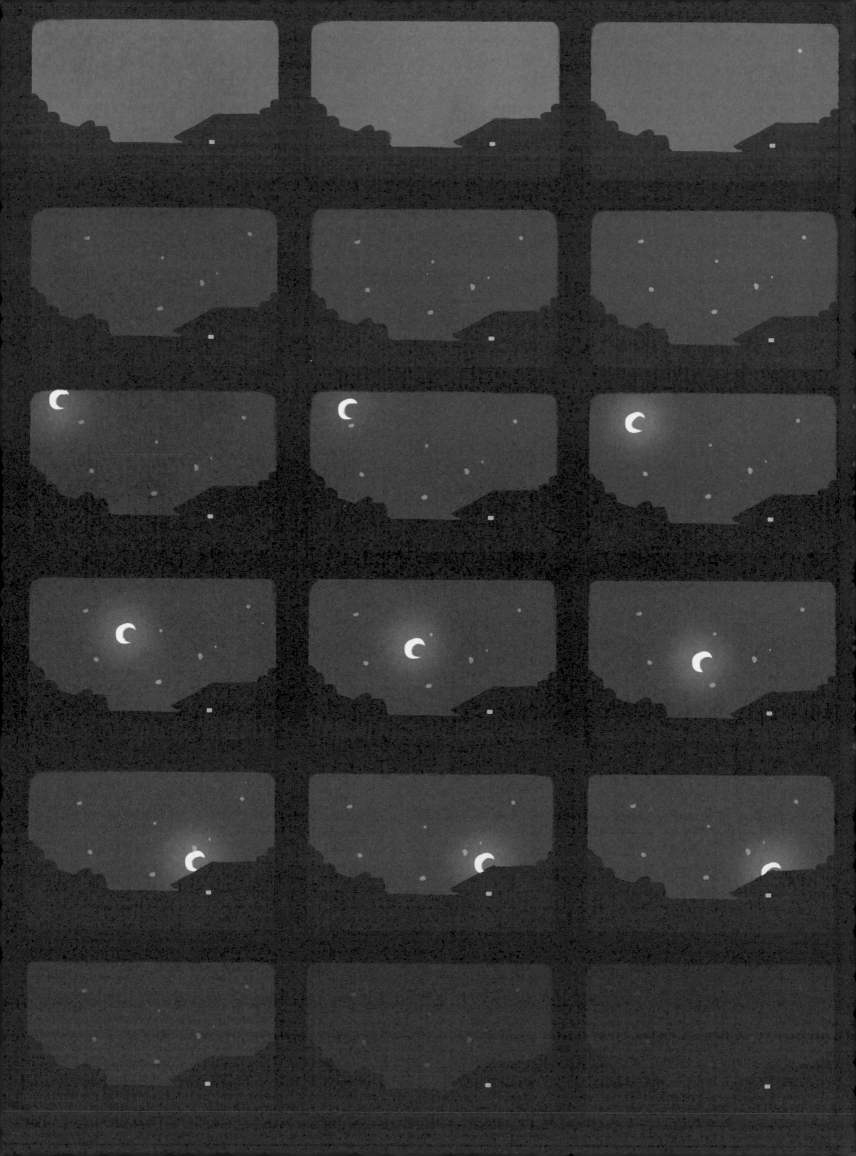